Mrs. Feathergreen Might Be a

SUPERHERO

BrainSmart
ACADEMICS

We dedicate this book to all teachers who have devoted their career to making a difference and promoting success for children with learning disabilities.

Printed in the United States of America

First Printing, 2016

ISBN-13: 978-0692721698 (Brain Smart Academics, LLC)
ISBN-10: 069272169X

Brain Smart Academics, LLC
BrainSmartAcademics.com

Illustrations Copyright © Marlo Garnsworthy
Book design by Marlo Garnsworthy
www.WordyBirdStudio.com

Children's drawings Copyright © Jonquil Rasmussen

Charts designed by Aaron Welch, Big A Designs & Printing
www.BigAMarketing.com

Mrs. Feathergreen Might Be a

SUPERHERO

Patricia Gage PhD, Joyce B. Holmes EdD,
& Marlo Garnsworthy

BrainSmart
ACADEMICS

Foreword

It's the first day of fourth grade, and Max is excited to join Mrs. Feathergreen's class: for the first time, he will be in a regular class, instead of Special Ed. Before, when he tried to read, the letters and words were a mess on the page, like black sticks scattered on snow. Nothing much made sense. Now, he almost always remembers his letters and sounds, and he can sound out longer words most of the time. Max finds Mrs. Feathergreen's class is different to anything he has experienced: she plays soothing music to start each day; they have recess twice; and they use fun tools such as mnemonics to help them remember what they learn. Her classroom even has two frogs—and if there's anything Max loves, it's frogs. Max's best friend has warned him that Mrs. Feathergreen is not a softy like a feather, and she's sure not green, and Max is determined not to let her down.

The human brain is a universe of countless possibilities. However, we have to provide the experiences to shape it and see it grow and develop. Since we have determined through neuroscience how the brain learns, it has become essential that we make every effort to apply these findings in the everyday teaching practices used in our children's classrooms. Brain compatible schools are able to provide opportunities for all learners to succeed.

We have discovered in recent years how emotions affect learning, memory, and recall, and how movement and exercise improve our mood and play a part in our emotional wellness, increase brain mass, and enhance cognitive processing. This story depicts the challenges a student with learning disabilities faces when he is first included and transitioned into a regular education classroom. Through his courage, his perseverance, and the efforts of his highly effective teacher, he is able to overcome his insecurities and self-doubts and achieve the successful classroom experience he seeks.

The book will be useful for classroom teachers because it demonstrates research-based instructional strategies that may be considered to increase the likelihood that successful learning will occur. College instructors should also find it a useful tool in demonstrating how research findings can be applied in the classroom. Parents are children's first set of teachers. A book like this can be a good starting point in facilitating their child's learning. Hence, learning challenges do not have to be looked upon as barriers to any child's academic success.

This book is a labor of love, and the culmination of our hard work over thirty years of testing, teaching, and advocating for students with disabilities.

Patricia P. Gage, PhD
Joyce B. Holmes, EdD

Chapter 1

As the school bus chugged away from my stop, I stared out at the pouring rain. It was my first day in fourth grade. My stomach was filled with worms, and they were doing massive backflips. I jumped as someone tapped my shoulder.

It was my buddy, Louis, and he was grinning.

"Hey, Max, whose class are you in this year?" he asked.

"Mrs. Feathergreen's," I said.

"Me too!" We high-fived, but then Louis looked serious.

"My sister had her last year," he said. "You know what Nicki said about her?"

Louis looked so grim, I was worried. "What?"

"She said Mrs. Feathergreen's name is all wrong. She's not a softy like a feather," said Louis. "And she's sure not green."

"What do you mean 'green'?" I knew he couldn't mean green like pickles or frogs.

"I mean, she knows her stuff, and she takes no nonsense. Nicki said she makes you work really hard."

I sighed. "Well that's nothing new." My last teacher, Miss Pearce, made me work hard, too. "Mom says I'm lucky to have Mrs. Feathergreen, but now I'm not so sure."

Louis shrugged then stared out at the gloomy morning, not looking sure, either. The rain was getting heavier, and the sky was dark and windy. I wished I were at home on the couch, drawing in my sketchbook.

Art is my favorite subject, followed by Recess, and then PE. My least favorite subject is Language Arts. Last year, spelling was like fighting an evil supervillain—difficult, messy, and not very successful. I usually passed the spelling tests, but as soon as the test was done, most of the words flew out of my brain. If I tried to write them in sentences, I spelled them wrong every time.

Whoever created the alphabet must not have liked kids very much. I mean, who can remember the difference between b and d? Or p and q? Sometimes you just have to guess and hope for the best. But would that be good enough in my new class?

By the time the bus pulled up outside school, my palms were all sweaty. As the door squeaked open, my heart pounded. I gulped, watching kids running through the rain into the building. I wasn't only thinking about Mrs. Feathergreen and my spelling and writing. I had other problems to worry about. What about the other kids in my new class? What would they think of me?

As I walked through the doors, I knew there was no going back now. At long last, I was going to be in a regular class. Mrs. No-Nonsense Feathergreen's class.

Chapter 2

I stood in the crowded hallway and took a deep breath.

"I have to take this to Nurse Judy," said Louis, holding up a baggie with his asthma medicine. "I'll see you in Mrs. Feathergreen's class."

"Ok," I said, wishing I didn't have to find the way alone.

Since kindergarten, I have had a different classroom to most kids in my grade. I didn't even know what "learning disabilities" meant when I was little, but by second grade, I knew I wasn't the same as most other kids. I couldn't learn some things as fast as them. Sometimes it made me feel frustrated. A lot of times, I felt embarrassed.

And other times, when the work was really hard, it made me mad—so mad I felt like throwing my papers onto the floor or snapping my pencil. At those times, Miss Pearce would say, "Max, you *must* learn to control your temper!" Boy, I hate getting in trouble.

But it wasn't always like that. Miss Pearce and her assistant were super nice most of the time. They took turns teaching me to read and write, and they gave me extra help whenever I needed it. Which was often. I must have made their job really difficult.

Every time I tried to read, the letters were scattered on the line. I couldn't connect them to words; they were like black twigs on snow. The letters and words got all mixed up. Nothing made much sense.

"But I've gotten better," I thought as I walked toward the fourth grade hallway. I suddenly felt excited about meeting Mrs. Feathergreen. No way was I going to let her down.

Someone had put four signs in the shape of arrows on the wall of the fourth grade hallway. Kids were reading them and then going toward different classrooms. I guessed the signs must say each teacher's name and point toward his or her classroom. When I got close, I saw I was right.

I peered at the arrows. It used to be that when I tried to sound out words, I couldn't remember which letters made which sounds. I practiced and practiced, but I just didn't get it.

You probably know there are twenty-six letters in the alphabet. But did you know there are forty-four sounds in the English language?

It's true. And there are only so many hours in the day. I forget

how many; I just know there are not enough hours to remember everything.

"You're in a regular class now," I told myself. "And you're a much better reader…" But I was afraid I would make a mistake and end up in the wrong classroom. That would be so embarrassing. I looked around for Louis, but he wasn't anywhere in sight.

"Fea-ther-green," I slowly sounded out her name. I studied the writing on the arrows. Feathergreen started with F, but so did two other names.

"Oh brother," I mumbled.

My eyes moved too fast as I stared at the letters. It all started to blur. I looked away then back to try again.

"Come on, Max," I thought. "You're just nervous. You can do this. You have to."

I picked the shortest name and sounded it out: Mr. F-E-A-R. Fear? I shuddered. I sure was glad I didn't get him! The next name was more difficult. It was longer, and it started with F-I-N-K. I knew it had to be Mrs. Finkelstein. Last year, I tripped over my shoelace and fell right into her classroom. Everybody laughed, and I felt like a real dummy, but she was really kind.

There was only one other name starting with F. It had to be Mrs. Feathergreen's. That's what movie detectives call working something out "by the process of elimination." But I sounded the word out anyway, just to be sure.

Mrs. F-E-A-T-H-E-R-G-R-E-E-N.

Feathergreen—I read it! The "feather" part wasn't that easy, but the "green" part was. Her classroom was to my left.

"Good job, dude," I told myself as I headed left down the hall. I remembered my letters and sounds most of the time now. I was getting better at sounding out bigger words. I only guessed once in a while, and I was way better at catching my mistakes. I was so glad Miss Pearce didn't give up on me.

Inside the classroom with "Mrs. Feathergreen" on the sign was a teacher. She turned and gave me a big smile.

"Good morning!" she said. "Nice to meet you, Max."

My throat was dry. My mouth was stuck shut, like I'd eaten too much peanut butter. How did she know my name? Did Miss Pearce tell her about me? Did she warn Mrs. Feathergreen? I couldn't say a single word. Mrs. Feathergreen smiled until I finally squeaked out, "Good morning."

Miss Pearce never gave up on me, but if I made too many mistakes, what would Mrs. Feathergreen do?

Chapter 3

"Come on in," said Mrs. Feathergreen.

My heart was thumping as I stepped into the classroom. The first thing I saw, right by the window, was a fish tank. Cool! The next thing I noticed was that music was playing.

"Am I in the wrong room? Is this the music class?" I blurted out. I felt terrible. Maybe I read the sign wrong after all.

"You're in the right room," she said. "My name is Mrs. Feathergreen. Welcome to fourth grade!"

I just nodded. I couldn't think of a single thing to say. "Would you like a high-five, or may I shake your hand?" she asked.

I probably would have asked for a high-five when I was in kindergarten, maybe even in first and second grade. But I was in fourth grade now. I put out my hand, just like my parents do when they meet someone.

Mrs. Feathergreen took my hand and shook it. I'd never shaken hands with an adult before. It made me feel very mature,

almost grownup. I stood up straighter and swallowed nervously, trying to think of something grownup to say.

"Why don't you look around while we wait for the others?" she said.

Phew. I wandered around, looking at the math and science posters and computers. I got excited at the art center: markers, paints, pencils, pastels, paper in all the colors of the rainbow, even glitter glue! But I saved the best for last. I went over to study the fish tank. Actually, it wasn't really a fish tank. It was filled with plants and rocks and some water. Inside were two greenish spotted African Dwarf Frogs.

If there are three things I like, they are drawing, space, and amphibians of all kinds—frogs, toads, newts, and salamanders. I also like reptiles like snakes, lizards, and crocodiles. Mrs. Feathergreen's class seemed pretty cool so far.

The worms in my stomach were settling down now. The music made me feel like I was floating. It rolled up and down with a slow, quiet beat that reminded me of something—it was like a heartbeat, but much calmer than mine. But apart from the music, the classroom was quiet. I was still the only kid there.

"Are you *sure* I'm in the right class?" I asked.

Mrs. Feathergreen just chuckled as other kids started pouring in, and soon the room was bustling. There were so many kids compared to Miss Pearce's class. I knew some of them, and they were nice. I waved to Louis, who waved back and grinned. But I wasn't too pleased to see Joey Jackson. That kid drives me nuts.

Mrs. Feathergreen asked us to sit in a circle on the rug, so I avoided Joey and sat between Louis and Li Mei.

"Good morning, everybody," Mrs. Feathergreen said. "I'm so excited to have you in my class. It's going to be the best school year ever!" After telling us a few rules, she said, "In my class, expect to hear pleasant music as we start and end our day."

I nudged Louis. "Maybe she's happy to see us come and happy to see us go again," I whispered. Louis sniggered.

Somehow Mrs. Feathergreen heard us. Still smiling, she said, "Yes, Max?"

Oh brother. Louis's sister was right. And Mrs. Feathergreen must have bionic hearing. "Um," I said, my face rocket red, "I was wondering, can I bring some music to play?"

"We have to carefully choose the music we listen to," said Mrs. Feathergreen. "It's important that the music have sixty beats a minute, just like a healthy human heart."

I was right about the music sounding like a heartbeat. "But it doesn't have any words," I blurted then suddenly felt shy again.

"I like music with words, too," said Mrs. Feathergreen. "But we start our school day with wordless music. That helps us pay attention. If we wanted to feel excited and jump around the room, what kind of music could we choose?" she asked.

Joey Jackson's hand shot up. "Fast music! Loud music! Dance music!" He shot out of his chair and did a jerky dance right there beside his desk. Everyone, even Mrs. Feathergreen laughed. It was funny, I guess. Especially the bit when she told him to sit back down.

"Sometimes, such as after recess when we need to quiet down, we'll play slower music with only forty to fifty beats per minute," she said. "We can't use music with lyrics, or loud, fast music, because it won't help us concentrate on our work."

Oh yeah, work. The thing I was *not* looking forward to.

"Now everybody, please find the desk with your name and put away your things." She didn't mind if we talked to each other, as long as we weren't too loud.

I walked along the lines of desks, looking for my name. (It's easy to read and write. It only has three letters.) I found it on a desk by the window. And guess what? It was right near the frog tank. Awesome! I put away my pencils, binder, brand-new markers, and my sketchbook. Maybe, if we had free time, I could draw the frogs. So far so good.

That's when I realized who was sitting beside me. Joey Jackson. He was really in my space. Then he leaned away toward the tank.

"Hello, little froggies," he said in a silly voice, reaching so far over he could tap on the glass. Frogs hate that.

"Oh *brother*," I said.

Mrs. Feathergreen asked us to take out a sheet of paper. "Please write down three things about yourself that you want your classmates to know."

Double oh brother.

Chapter 4

I stared at the lines on the paper, thinking. It was hard enough to think of three things to share—but three things I *wanted* to share? All I could think of was that this was my first day in a regular class, and no way did I want to share that. I didn't want anyone to know I had a learning disability, not even Mrs. Feathergreen. Make that *especially* not Mrs. Feathergreen. Plus, I had to choose something easy to write because I felt so nervous.

So I wrote:

I like bogs.

"No, dummy," I thought. It wasn't right. But I remembered what Miss. Pearce said—that I should never call anyone a "dummy" and especially not myself. I erased what I wrote, gripped my pencil, and wrote more carefully this time.

I like dogs.

I stopped frowning. Like I said, b and d are confusing. Actually, I like bogs, too, because that's where you'll find a bunch of frogs. (And like I said, I really like amphibians.)

I erased again and wrote slowly.

I like frogs that live in dogs.

Oooops. I crossed out *dogs* and wrote *bogs*.

I was feeling pretty clever now. I even smiled a little bit. Mrs. Feathergreen was going to love this... Then I erased it all. Probably, the other kids would think frogs in bogs were stupid. I tried to write about the water park I went to during the summer and eating a whole pepperoni pizza all by myself. Except I didn't even try to spell "pepperoni," and I couldn't remember if it was "hole" with an "h," or "whole" with a "w." I just knew I'd made lots of mistakes.

When we were finished, Mrs. Feathergreen had Maria collect our papers. But then she got to Joey, who was still writing. Maria looked over his shoulder.

"*I lick newts,*" she read loudly. "Ewwwwww. You *lick* them? That's so gross, Joey."

I tried not to giggle. I couldn't help it.

"I *like* them," muttered Joey. Now *his* face was rocket red.

"Still disgusting," huffed Maria. "Totally gross."

I knew how Joey felt. I quickly folded my paper so Maria

21

wouldn't read it, too.

But right then, Mrs. Feathergreen said, "Time for recess! Please line up quietly by the door once you've handed Maria your paper."

The bell hadn't even rung. Everyone began to talk and laugh. As we were walking out of the classroom, I thought, "We've only been in class for a little while, and we're already getting a break!" I couldn't believe my ears.

I guess a few us looked puzzled because Mrs. Feathergreen added, "We'll have recess twice a day. That's so you can move about and get some exercise. Exercise and fresh air will get oxygen to your brain. That will help you focus and do your best work."

I sure wasn't going to argue with that.

But then Joey Jackson pushed in front of me. I might have felt sorry for him for a second, but that guy was already getting on my nerves again.

Chapter 5

Joey Jackson is not my favorite person. Ever since kindergarten, he has been our grade's biggest bully. He makes fun of everyone. He gave us all nicknames in first grade, and they were pretty mean. Worse, they've stuck. Louis was "Loser," and I was "Booger-face." Don't expect me tell you why. I'm sure you can guess. He's *so* immature.

Even though the teachers often talked about being kind and helpful to each other, Joey still did it when no one was looking. Or so he thought. Joey has had to visit Principal Holiday too many times to count.

Like a lot of kids, Joey and I both like to play dodgeball during recess. He can always push my anger buttons, especially during dodgeball. Luckily, the rain had stopped. But as usual, the second the ball closet was opened, Joey pushed ahead of everybody. He grabbed the dodgeball, and once he had it, he wouldn't give it up.

"Pass the ball!" I said. "Give someone else a turn."

"Why should I?" sneered Joey. "If you're all too slow to get it, that's too bad. Get over it, Booger-face."

"Stay calm, Max," I told myself and slumped toward the sideline. "You don't want to get in trouble on your first day."

Joey just took over. He didn't give anyone a turn. Kids were calling him a "ball hog" and worse under their breath, but nobody did anything about it. Finally, I got to play again.

"Hey, Max, catch!" said Stephanie when the ball rolled her way.

But as usual, Joey jumped in and grabbed it. Then he threw it.

"Oww!" I was out and probably had the bruise to prove it. "That was mine!" I said.

Joey shrugged. "Too bad. I got it first. Now it's mine. *Again.*"

I got soooooo mad. I felt my face turn hot and red, just like a cartoon character with an anvil dropped on his foot. Steam shot out of my ears, I bet. Before I even knew it, I had pushed Joey—hard.

He fell to the ground with a grunt. "Ow! Ow!" he wailed, holding his left knee. What a faker.

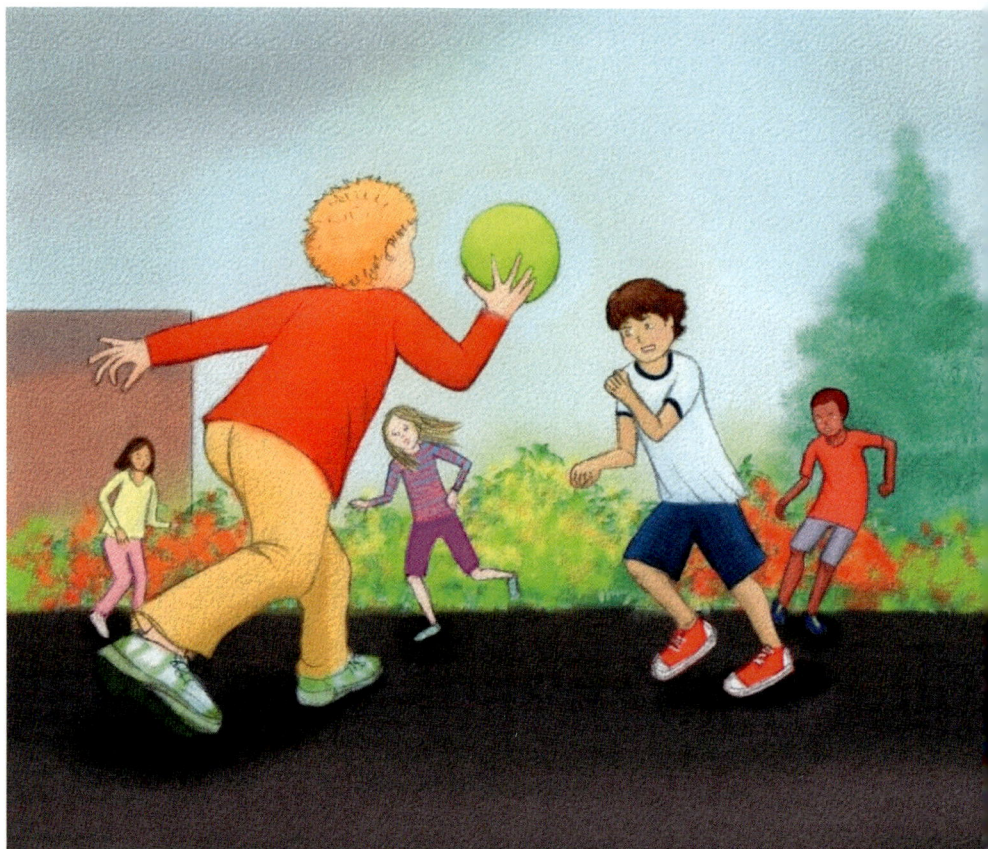

But too bad for me. Mrs. Feathergreen must have eyes in the back of her head as well as bionic hearing. I bet they're like the Hubble Space telescope—able to see beyond the galaxy, or at least way across the blacktop.

She was coming right toward us.

Chapter 6

Oh man… I stomped off and sat on a bench at the far end of the blacktop. I wouldn't look at anybody.

Mrs. Feathergreen would be so mad. I knew she was going to say, "Max, you *must* learn to control your temper!" I might even have to see Principal Holiday. He'd probably call my parents, and they'd be angry, too. I'd lose my computer and TV privileges for sure. I was in *big* trouble. Capital B-I-G *big*.

I've blown it, I thought. *Should I even be in this class?* Maybe I'd be sent back to my old class. A line of ants was crawling along the damp ground near my foot. I felt about as big as an ant—but with a lot fewer friends.

I had been so proud to be in a regular class at last. I hated the thought of going back.

While I was busy feeling sorry for myself, footsteps came along the blacktop toward me. I didn't need to look up to know they were Mrs. Feathergreen's. I stared at the ants, wishing I could follow them into the hole in the ground.

The footsteps stopped in front of me. To my surprise, a gentle hand lay on my shoulder. But I couldn't look up.

"How do you feel, Max?"

I didn't expect to hear that. I didn't say anything. I didn't know what to say.

"Max?" Mrs. Feathergreen wasn't going to give up.

I remembered what Louis said on the bus: "Mrs. Feathergreen is not a softy like a feather. And she's sure not green." I knew I had to answer—and I had better be completely honest.

"MAD," I said a bit louder than I meant to. "I feel really *mad*."

Mrs. Feathergreen sat down beside me. "We all get mad sometimes," she said, peering down at the ants. "Hmmm. I really like ants. Look how they're working as a team to carry that breadcrumb."

I dared a quick look at her. Her green eyes were kind. And she didn't look or sound angry.

"Aren't you mad at me?" I asked, staring at the ants again.

But before she could answer, Joey hopped over holding his knee. He wobbled to a stop in front of us, whining, "Mrs. Feathergreen, Max pushed me for no reason. He broke my dermis. Owwww, it hurts so badly!"

"Did not! It's not—" I started to shout, but then I stopped. What if his dermis was broken? And what was a dermis? What if it was serious? I didn't want to make things worse.

"Did too!" yelled Joey.

Mrs. Feathergreen examined his grubby knee. "Your skin—

your dermis—doesn't seem to be broken, Joey. Recess is almost over. Please collect the balls and other equipment for me," she said firmly. "You and I will speak later."

Joey scowled, but he stomped away just fine and did as he was told. I couldn't help smirking a little.

Mrs. Feathergreen looked at me. "You know, Max, it's okay to feel angry," she said.

"It is?" I said.

"Yes," said Mrs. Feathergreen, "but…"

"Of course there had to be a 'but.'"

"*But*," Mrs. Feathergreen continued, "taking your anger out on other people is not okay."

"I know," I mumbled.

"Anger is a very strong feeling. It's important we learn how to handle such strong feelings in a positive way."

I nodded, but I felt like pushing Joey all over again.

"Why don't you try taking a little Brain Break?" she said. "That will help you feel calm."

"A Brain Break?" I asked. "What's that?"

"I want you to take some deep breaths with me. Let's try it," she said. "Breathe in slowly through your nose, and out through your mouth just as slowly." I did, while Mrs. Feathergreen counted, "In, 2, 3, 4…Out, 2, 3, 4."

As I slowly breathed in and out, I started to feel a little calmer. My face didn't feel so hot, and my heart wasn't pounding hard anymore.

Mrs. Feathergreen said, "Make sure you fill your belly with air—just like a balloon." Then I saw Joey punch the ball Louis was carrying out his hands. I felt my head about to pop—just like a balloon.

I guess Mrs. Feathergreen saw. "If that doesn't help, use some positive 'self-talk,'" she said. "Say, 'I'm calm. I can do it.'"

"I'm calm. I can do it," I said through gritted teeth. But because of Joey Jackson, I might be back in Miss Pearce's class.

"Or if that still doesn't work," said Mrs. Feathergreen, "you can count backwards from thirty to one."

I tried it. I had to really concentrate, so I stopped watching Joey. I stared at the sky instead. The rainclouds were clearing, and there was the faintest rainbow in the sky. I pointed at it, and Mrs. Feathergreen smiled.

I guess I did a good job of distracting my brain from thinking about Joey the Jerk because, before I knew it, I almost forgot I'd been angry.

But Mrs. Feathergreen didn't forget.

Chapter 7

We had just sat down again, when Mrs. Feathergreen stood up behind her desk. Her face was very serious. I felt Joey's glare poking holes in the side of my head.

"I'm calling a class meeting," Mrs. Feathergreen announced. She even had a gavel, just like a real judge. She banged it on her desk with a thump. "We've had some incidents on the playground where kids did things that were unsafe and hurtful."

Joey was fake sniveling beside me. But I was so glad Mrs. Feathergreen didn't say our names.

"When someone upsets you, it's normal to feel angry," said Mrs. Feathergreen. "But how you handle your anger is what's important. Instead of hurting someone back, what could you do? When you think of something, please raise your hand."

Since I'd just spent recess practicing breathing with Mrs. Feathergreen, I considered myself an expert. Also, I would

Take a Brain Break!
-Take slow, deep breaths
-Count backwards from 39 to 1
-Tell them how you feel
-Listen to soft, calm music

show Joey. I held my hand up high.

"Yes, Max?" said Mrs. Feathergreen.

"You can breathe slowly and deeply. Or you can count backwards from thirty to one, until you're calm."

Mrs. Feathergreen smiled. "Excellent suggestions for how to handle anger, Max. Good job."

I let out my breath in a *whoosh*. I shot my hand up again.

"Max?"

"You can step away from whatever is happening. You can take a Brain Break until you feel calm."

Mrs. Feathergreen wrote my suggestions on the board. Joey shifted in his seat. His anger felt like laser beams.

Then Stephanie chimed in, "You can tell the person how they're making you feel. You can ask them not to do it again."

"Yes," said Mrs. Feathergreen, "you can use an 'I statement.' Use the person's name, and say, 'I don't like it when you do that.' Tell the person how it makes you feel. Use your strong voice, but don't be mean or rude."

"You can listen to some music," said Louis. "I like rock music."

"That works well, too," added Mrs. Feathergreen, "but it's even better if you listen to soft, calming music without lyrics."

"You can play music, too," said Rakeem, sitting in the front. "When my little brother bugs me, which is pretty much all the time, I crash the piano keys really hard. But soon, I slow down and play a nice tune. It always makes me feel better."

Maria put up her hand. "You can think about something that makes you happy," she said. "Something you really love— like puppies."

"Or unicorns," added Stephanie, Maria's best friend. They both love puppies. And unicorns.

"Or unicorn puppies," Maria said.

"Uni-puppies," said Stephanie. Then they giggled. Girls are *so* weird.

"Oh, I really like that idea," laughed Mrs. Feathergreen. "I may try thinking about uni-puppies myself."

"When I'm mad, I ride my bike around," said Justin. "Sometimes I go out in my yard and shoot some baskets."

"You all have great suggestions," said Mrs. Feathergreen. She had written all our ideas on the board.

Joey was knocking my chair with his knee. I noticed he hadn't made any suggestions. Then he was nudging my chair with his foot, not loud enough to hear, but hard enough to be really annoying. Obviously, he was still trying to get me back. I took a deep breath and ignored him.

"Remember, you can always come and talk with me about a problem, too," said Mrs. Feathergreen. "You can trust me with your feelings."

But could I really trust her with my feelings? Maybe. She hadn't sent me to the principal. But she still might call my parents. I still might get sent back to Miss Pearce's class. I just didn't know.

Chapter 8

"Time for lunch," said Mrs. Feathergreen as the bell rang.

Lunch is my favorite time of day. Today was especially nice because I got to sit next to Stephanie and Maria, which took my mind off the cafeteria food.

The spaghetti looked like guts, and it smelled like sweaty socks. But we were having too much fun drawing uni-puppies in my sketchbook to care.

We decided to give one to Mrs. Feathergreen.

When we walked into the classroom after lunch, a song with lyrics was playing. I realized it was about the states. It started with Alabama and ended with Wyoming. Mrs. Feathergreen was singing all the words. Her voice sounded really pretty.

"Wow, she can really sing, too," I thought, handing her our drawing. She said she loved it and stuck it on the wall next to her desk!

"Today we'll review the states and capitals and see what you remember. Then, we'll start learning the different countries around the world and their capitals.

I'm so bad at memorizing things, I thought. *This is going to be a nightmare. Everyone will find out how bad I am!*

"This is one of my favorite things to teach," Mrs. Feathergreen said. "Today we will begin to learn our states and their capitals. We'll learn songs like this one to help us remember them. Who knows the capital of our state?" she asked.

Most kids raised their hands, but I kept my eyes down. I knew it was a long name, but I couldn't remember what it was. Before Mrs. Feathergreen could call on anyone, Joey shouted, "Tallahassee!"

"That's right, Joey, but next time, I expect you to raise your hand. Please wait to be called on before you speak."

I didn't even feel pleased. How was I ever going to remember that name?

"Here's a fun way to remember. Picture a dog, Lassie, with a towel in her mouth. Picture her mopping the floor." On the board, Mrs. Feathergreen wrote:

Floor = Florida.
Towel + Lassie = Tallahassee.

"I want you to picture this and say it to yourselves a few times. This is an example of a 'mnemonic'—a little trick to help us remember things. Today, I'll assign each of you a state. You will research the name of the capital and come up with your own mnemonic, or a silly sentence, to teach the class."

mnemonics
ne-mon-ix

Brussels, Belgium

Tallahassee

towel + Lassie

I liked this kind of memorizing. It's a lot easier to learn when I see a picture of something, but it also helps to say things out loud a few times. I wondered if Mrs. Feathergreen knew that about me already.

She walked down each row of desks, handing out papers. I started to get squirmy worms in my stomach again. What if I couldn't read it?

Turns out everyone liked that assignment. Lucy called from the back, "I got one for Juneau, Alaska. Too cold to go to Alaska except in June."

Next to her, Matthew said, "I have a funny one for Springfield, Illinois. You can't spring out of bed if you're ill."

"I have another funny one for you," said Mrs. Feathergreen. "Some of you might prefer drawing things you want to remember. A while back, a student came up with a really clever visual to help her remember that Brussels is the capital of the country Belgium. Picture this: She associated the word Brussels with Brussels sprouts and the word Belgium with Belgian waffles. What did she draw? Can you guess?"

Quick as anything, while she was still talking, I drew a picture of evil green Brussels sprouts on top of scared looking waffles. I held it up.

"I bet she'll never forget that capital," chuckled Mrs. Feathergreen.

"Neither will we," said Louis, and everyone laughed.

Me? I got Washington State. I couldn't believe it. I already knew the capital is Olympia because that's where my uncle lives. I've even been there! It rained every single day.

Washington made me think of George Washington. And Olympia made me think of the Olympics. My mnemonic was "George Washington won a medal at the Olympics." Mrs. Feathergreen liked that a lot.

Joey got the easiest one of all. Oklahoma. The capital of Oklahoma is Oklahoma City. Who could forget that?

Some guys get all the breaks.

Chapter 9

Two days later, Mrs. Feathergreen put our first spelling list up on the board. When I saw how long it was and how hard the words were, those worms started wriggling in my stomach again.

"Please copy these words into your spelling notebook," said Mrs. Feathergreen. "We will study the hardest five words today, the next hardest five tomorrow, and so on until Thursday. We will review all the words together before our spelling test."

Here we go, I thought. *I'll have to write the words three times each, make silly sentences, and who knows what else now I'm in a regular class.*

Shaking, I picked up my pencil in my left hand. I sighed and leaned on my right hand, accidentally bumping Joey's arm.

"Look whatcha made me do," said Joey, pointing to the pencil streak across his work.

"Geez, I didn't mean to," I said. "I couldn't help it."

"Because you're a lefty," sniggered Joey. "Look at the weird way you're holding your pencil, Twisty-hand Booger-face."

"So?"

So *what* if I'm a lefty? But boy, I get sick of kids making fun of how I hold my pencil. It works for me. Well sort of. My handwriting is nothing to brag about, but it's readable. Mostly.

So I said, "Did you know that three quarters of the last four presidents have been lefties?"

That shut him up! (I silently thanked Miss Pearce for teaching me *that* comeback.)

Besides super vision, bionic hearing, and an awesome singing voice, Mrs. Feathergreen must also have mindreading skills. When she saw me writing, she came over and looked at my notebook.

I wanted to throw my hands over it, but I didn't. I kind of mix the lower case with the upper case letters. Sometimes the size of the letters is pretty different, and I usually end up with double strokes on my O's. That's what happens when I make some of my letters from the bottom up, instead of top to bottom like we're supposed to.

"You know, Max, in our class we use a special and fun writing program. It gives us good cues that help us remember how to make letters neatly. For example, look at the magic letter c. It helps form the letters a, b, c, g, o, and q."

She said it quietly, but I knew Joey heard every word. But he wasn't sneering or even writing. He seemed to be listening very carefully. I had a feeling there were two things coming: more tips from Mrs. Feathergreen and more of Joey being a total meanoid.

"You can also go to these websites and play games to practice your words," Mrs. Feathergreen told the class, handing out a list of website addresses. Louis gave me a thumbs up.

"And here is a mnemonic that you will find really helpful for this week's spelling words." On the board she wrote,

"If you're unsure whether a word is spelled with *ie* or *ei*, say this mnemonic to yourself."

She gave us some examples from our spelling list:

ie	*ei*
believe	*ceiling*
fierce	*deceive*
friend	*receipt*

I thought that was a really helpful mnemonic! I started to feel much better about spelling.

"By the end of the week, you'll write sentences using your spelling words and share them with the class." She also gave us the choice to record our sentences first and then play them back as many times as we needed to get it all down on paper.

Ok, Max, I told myself. *You've got this.*

"Each year, all my junior authors write such clever and interesting sentences, and I know yours will be, too. I'll even have you illustrate them with colorful pictures."

I knew what I was going to write my sentences about already. A <u>fierce</u> freckle-faced monster who licks newts, and is not a <u>friend</u>. The monster tries to <u>deceive</u> Booger-Man, the superhero who swoops around the <u>ceiling</u> in his red rocket ship. I glanced at Joey and grinned to myself.

"What?" said Joey with a dirty mean scowl. "Keep your eyes on your *own* work." He threw his arms over his page.

But it was too late. I saw what he was trying to hide. His handwriting was pretty bad, maybe way worse than mine. I couldn't believe we had something in common.

Chapter 10

By the time I got off the bus that day, I had my sentences all worked out in my head. Then I realized I'd need to start the writing part sooner or later. Ugh! Homework! I always worked so slowly. I drifted off to outer space all the time. Homework took *forever.*

Last year, I also had trouble remembering to bring home the textbooks and notebooks I needed. I didn't always understand what Miss Pearce taught me, so sometimes I couldn't do it anyway. Even when I did my homework, I couldn't find it when I got to school. Sometimes I just forgot to hand it in. I was getting zeroes left and right for incomplete homework and notes saying "unsatisfactory" or "needs improvement." My parents always nagged me or talked together quietly, looking worried.

Before I knew it, Mrs. Feathergreen assigned me a "homework buddy"—someone I could call after school with

homework questions. But it was Louis, because Mrs. Feathergreen let me choose, and Louis was really cool with that, too. But one thing wasn't Ok.

Obviously, my new teacher already had plans for me before she even met me. Miss Pearce must have spilled the beans to Mrs.

Feathergreen. I didn't know how I felt about either of them right then.

At the end of the following day, Mrs. Feathergreen gave us ten minutes before the bell to pack up and take out our planners. "Check what assignments you've written in your planner against what's on the board. Make sure it's correct." She initialed our planners when we were done.

"I won't be checking your planner all the time," she said, "just until you get in the habit."

I remembered something. I put up my hand.

"Yes, Max?"

"If you do something thirty times in a row, it becomes a habit. Then you can do it without trying so hard or being reminded all the time."

"Max, that's so interesting! And it's also very helpful for all of us to hear. Thanks for sharing it with the class."

I smiled, remembering this at home after school. I was eating my favorite snack—banana smeared with peanut butter—as slowly as I could. I wanted to put off my homework for as long as I could. I had remembered that fact about habits because Miss Pearce taught me. And Mrs. Feathergreen was grateful for me sharing it. I decide to forgive them both for talking about me.

That first week in Mrs. Feathergreen's class was fun. She was always thinking up something new, and so far, I was keeping up.

Some days, she let me only do half the math problems, only the odd numbers on the sheet. "As long as you show me you know how to do them," she said.

Sometimes she allowed me extra time to do my work, and she gave me more time to take our first spelling test on Friday. She must have noticed I do better if I have more time to get my answers down on paper or reread the questions and my answers—or maybe Miss Pearce told her. That's Ok. With the extra time, I was getting a lot better at catching my mistakes.

Joey had been ignoring me while he worked, and I was happy ignoring him, too. I won't say the worms in my stomach were gone, but they sure were quieter.

But the end of each day was still crazy. I kept forgetting stuff: which binder to take, leaving my homework in my cubby, even my planner, which a parent was supposed to sign each day. It made homework time a nightmare and the worms in my stomach turn into snakes.

Chapter 11

By Monday the next week, Mrs. Feathergreen had figured out that most kids were still having trouble remembering what to take home. She didn't make us feel bad about it. Instead, she made us a sign to tape inside our lockers.

When I stood in front of my locker, anxious about getting a bus seat next to Louis and trying to concentrate in all the noise, the sign was a good reminder! But the next day, it just felt like a lot to handle. I didn't even look at the locker checklist, even though it was staring me in the face. I just wanted to get outside and act like it was still the weekend.

I guess there were other kids who felt the same way, so the next day, Mrs. Feathergreen tried to sweeten the deal. She gave us a chance to earn extra privileges if we showed her we were trying a little harder to carry out our "responsibilities" as she calls them.

BEFORE I LEAVE SCHOOL CHECKLIST

☐ I have my home and school folder.

☐ My planner is complete for each class/subject assignments.

☐ I understand all assignments and know the due dates.

☐ I have all necessary books, notebooks, materials, and supplies.

☐ I spoke to all necessary persons.

☐ I reviewed my "to-do" list.

Nature #22
Poison Dart Frog

Nature #79
American Toad

She also made up a "behavior chart" just for me. It was supposed to help me stay more organized and be more "responsible." She even asked me what I thought I needed to do to get better. Then she showed me how to do each thing on my list.

I'll never remember all of this, I thought, *or worse, I'll do something to lose my checkmarks. Why bother?*

Mrs. Feathergreen's super mind-reading powers sprang into action. "I don't expect you to earn all your checkmarks every day, but if you don't have a good day, you don't lose any checkmarks you've already earned; you just don't get any new ones that day. Remember, every day is a new day—you get to try all over again."

It seemed simple. I'd get a checkmark every time I did what I was supposed to, so long as she only had to ask me once. When I got most of the checkmarks, I could earn special privileges from my very own menu.

"On Fridays," she said, "the weekly chart will go home to your parents. Together, you'll decide if you earned your special treat for your hard work and effort. I know you can do it."

Right then, I felt I could. I was determined that each week, I'd get more checkmarks than the week before. It would be like a game.

Mrs. Feathergreen also said she'd check in with my parents. I was anxious about what she'd say, until I got home.

Here's what I chose!

Celebration Menu

_____ Computer/iPad Time

_____ Bake Cookies with Mom

_____ Play a Board Game with Dad

_____ Sleepover with a Friend

_____ Cook My Favorite Meal

_____ Go Bowling

_____ Go Fishing

_____ _____

80% Compliance _____

Celebrate on _____

Mrs. Feathergreen must have said some nice stuff about me. Mom seemed less worried, even happy. She let me shoot baskets in our driveway with my neighbor, Juan, before starting my homework. While I was eating my snack, Mom sat with me.

"From now on, we'll use a timer when you do your homework. Plan to work hard for twenty minutes and then take a ten minute break until you're done."

"Really?" I said. "Can I play during the breaks?"

"Really, and yes you can play—except no screen-time."

I groaned.

"It will wait until your homework's done."

"Ok…" I grumbled. "Sounds like a pretty good deal."

"It will be—as long as I don't have to nag to get you back to your homework."

I really liked this plan. It kind of made me feel in charge. And ten minutes off was a great "Brain Break." Also, Mom didn't nag—not once. She didn't have to!

But after school the next day, things weren't so great. When I sat down and read my assignments, I couldn't remember what I was supposed to do. Thank goodness for homework buddies! Louis was really helpful, and I even helped him remember something *he* had forgotten!

Chapter 12

On Thursday, Mrs. Feathergreen handed out gigantic science books with endless pages. I couldn't believe we would read and learn all that in one school year. At least, there was a cool section about the solar system.

Mrs. Feathergreen didn't even give me a chance to feel sorry for myself. "Open your book to the first chapter, read the title, and ask yourself, 'What is this going to be about? What do I already know about this subject?'"

I opened my book, but Mrs. Feathergreen was still giving instructions.

"Then read the study questions in the back of the chapter first," she continued. "By reading the questions first, you'll get an idea of what's important and what you need to pay most attention to. It gives you the reason for reading and good clues about which details are important."

She had us take some sticky notes and start reading. As we read, we looked for the main idea and keywords in each section and added a sticky note to keep track of each important fact and questions we might have. I wanted to make sure I didn't miss anything. My first page was looking pretty yellow from all the sticky notes.

"Notice that some vocabulary words are in bold print. Note only keywords, not the whole sentence."

As I read, I realized there were a lot of vocabulary words I didn't know, but Mrs. Feathergreen had a super idea for that, too.

She gave us a stack of colorful index cards. "Write the word on one side and the definition on the other. Then imagine something that will remind you of its meaning and make a drawing."

While I tried to figure out what she meant, she wrote the word "descend" on the board. She drew a stick figure and, next to it, a line zig-zagging downward like stairs. She called it "using association" to help us understand and remember. I just knew I remember things better when I see a picture while I am learning something. Since I like to draw and I'm good at it, I thought this would be a breeze.

Mrs. Feathergreen said we would read the chapter aloud together and figure out the main ideas. We had to answer questions about *who* and *what* it was about. As if figuring out the

answers to these two W questions wasn't hard enough, Mrs. Feathergreen threw some more W's on the pile: Where? When? Why?

Our brains were now invaded by the five W's, and we couldn't rest until we answered them all. But she showed us an easier way to handle it. She gave us each five index cards, and this is what we wrote on them:

Who? Look for a person.
What? Look for an event.
Where? Look for a place.
When? Look for a time.
Why? Look for a reason.

"Put the cards on the left side of your desk," said Mrs. Feathergreen. "As we read, when you hear the 'who' or the 'why,' for example, move that card to the right, raise your hand, and tell the class." That sure made it easier and fun!

By then it was time for D.E.A.R., Drop Everything and Read. Reading, my greatest foe—or so I thought until Mrs. Feathergreen read to *us* for twenty minutes. And it was great! She read one of my favorite stories—*The Story of Ferdinand*, the bull who would rather smell flowers than fight. She also said we should each always have a book in our desk.

"As soon as you finish your classwork, you should read your book."

But then she said the scariest words she had said so far: "book report."

Chapter 13

My heart started to race. The snakes in my stomach transformed into anacondas, and they were having some kind of crazy snake dance party. It's not that I don't like books. I love looking at the pictures, and I like stories a lot. But a book report? I'd never done anything like that before. Not only would I have to finish reading a whole book, I'd have to write a report about it, too?

After she answered some questions, Mrs. Feathergreen took us to the library. Kids scattered, seeming excited to choose their books. I dawdled by the water fountain, taking extra big gulps.

The next thing I knew, Mrs. Feathergreen was beside me. "Max," she whispered, "I'll let you pick out your own book as long as you stay in the green section."

A huge weight lifted off my shoulders, and the snakes started to settle. I knew the easiest, shortest books were in the green section. Boy, was I relieved Mrs. Feathergreen always knew what was going on.

So I looked at the pictures, trying to find a book that looked interesting.

But wouldn't you know it? There was Joey, right where I wanted to be, pulling out books in the green section, too. Just as I reached for a cool looking book about amphibians, he grabbed it, too. And he wouldn't let it go.

"Hey, I saw it first," I said. I knew he was a ball-hog, but a book-hog? Oh boy.

"Did not," said Joey.

I tugged on the book. Joey yanked back. We stared each other down. My blood was starting to boil.

That Mrs. Feathergreen must have telepathic powers because I straightaway heard her voice in my mind. *Take a Brain Break, Max. Deep, slow belly breaths. In, 2, 3, 4…"* I took some slow, deep breaths in and out, but I did not let go of that book.

"Why don't you get a book from another section?" I asked, still holding on tightly.

"Because I can't!" hissed Joey, refusing to let go. "And I really like amphibians."

"Really?" I asked in surprise.

"Yeah," snapped Joey. "So what? I'm not *dumb*, you know. I

can read. And newts are cool." His chin wobbled a bit, as if he were about to cry. And this time, he wasn't faking.

Geez, I couldn't believe it: I felt sorry for the guy!

I know what it's like to feel embarrassed when you're not very good at something. I thought about Mrs. Feathergreen and everything we'd talked about. I took another long, deep breath in, and then I slowly let it out. We were both still gripping the book.

I had to take another deep breath in and out. And then another. I may even have counted backwards from thirty to one. But, finally, I let go of the book.

"I guess you really do like amphibians, huh?" I said.

He nodded. His chin had stopped wobbling, but he wouldn't look at me.

"I really like them, too."

"You do?" Joey did look at me then, and the frown fell off his face. He could see I was telling the truth.

I nodded. "Yeah. I like reptiles, including snakes, and space and also…"

Did I dare tell him?

"What?" said Joey.

I took another deep breath. "Well, I can't really read books in the other sections either."

He stared at me in surprise. "I bet you've never heard of poison dart frogs," he challenged at last.

"Have too. They're super colorful, and they come from the jungles of South America," I said. "They have deadly poison in their skin. I like the bright blue and black ones best. They're called okopipi. I always remember that name because it's funny."

"You know your frogs." Joey opened the book and found a picture of them. "They look like they're from outer space."

"Yeah, they sure do!" I agreed. Then I had a great idea. "Want to look at it together?"

That was when Mrs. Feathergreen came around the end of the book shelf and winked at me. I swear she has x-ray vision, too.

Chapter 14

So Joey and I looked at the frog book together. Turns out he knows his amphibians, too. Next we found a book about snakes. Did you know the anaconda is the biggest snake in the world? Joey was so excited, he handed *Amphibians of the World* to me.

"Hey, Booger, you can choose this, if you want," he said. "Then maybe we can swap them." Even if he's a ball hog, I guess Joey's not such a bad guy—when you get to know him.

When I got back to class, Mrs. Feathergreen asked me, "How many pages are in the book?"

"Forty pages," I answered. Oh brother, forty pages was a bunch! How would I ever get through them all?

"Please write in your planner that you will read five pages a day. You'll do this for the next eight school days, starting tomorrow. Each night, I want you to write a short summary, around five lines, about what you read."

For a moment, I felt that old feeling, like an evil supervillain was about to take me down. But then I took some slow belly breaths and stood up straight. I was in Mrs. Feathergreen's class now.

I shrugged. "That sounds fair. I can do that." And right then, I knew I really could.

At the end of the day, as I stood by my locker, carefully checking my list, Mrs. Feathergreen called my name.

"Max, before you read your book, I'd like you to listen to this once." She handed me a CD. "It's an audiobook of *Amphibians of the World*, so you can listen to it aloud. It will help you understand the book better and remember more information."

That was a cool idea. I like it when people read to me, and it's not as hard to remember things I hear.

"Once you finish the book," she added, "as a special treat, I'll let you take home a movie called *Invasion of the Cane Toads*. It's a true story."

"No way!" That sounded awesome. But there was still the problem of the book report.

Mrs. Feathergreen gave me and a couple of other kids, Joey included, the best deal. She suggested we each illustrate our favorite part of our book and make a poster sharing facts and information from it. "This will be instead of writing a book report," she said. That was a no-brainer for me, since drawing is my passion. Only a superhero teacher with the power to see inside people would think of that.

As it turns out, I'm not the only kid in Mrs. Feathergreen's class who takes longer to learn some things. I'm not the only one who loves amphibians and reptiles, either. Joey smiled at me, but it wasn't a mean smile. It was a smile that said, "Hey we have something else in common."

As Louis and I walked out to our bus that afternoon, the sun was beaming. "Mrs. Feathergreen is cool."

"I know!" said Louis. "I thought it would be all downhill after the first week. But it's fun."

"I wonder what tricks Mrs. Feathergreen has up her sleeve for next week," I said. "I can't wait!"

I didn't tell Louis I suspect Mrs. Feathergreen is a secret superhero. But we're both getting the picture: for Mrs. Feathergreen, failure is not an option. Like she always says, "Failure is only failure to try." I know failure is not an option for me, either.

Just before I got on the bus, I passed Joey. "Hey, dude," I said. "When I get that *Invasion of the Cane Toads* movie, wanna come over and watch it?"

"That would be cool, Max!" called Joey. I was no longer Booger-face.

That's when I saw Mrs. Feathergreen standing by the school doors, looking at us. She smiled her superhero smile and waved.

I think I like fourth grade!

The End

Behavior Plans Work!

Consistency and clearly stated rules and expectations are the key to positive discipline. Children need consistent positive feedback to learn and practice appropriate behaviors. Pay attention and notice the positive behaviors and reward your child often.

The focus needs to be on specific behaviors you want them to demonstrate, not on the behavior you want them to stop. Behavior charts are a fun and interactive way to encourage and motivate positive behavior.

Kids really like earning stickers or points, and you'll find they are willing to work for a special reward at the end of the week. Make the chart together and create the menu of things the child can select to work for each week.

Don't expect quick results. If the target behavior is very challenging for the child, start with 50% compliance. If the child demonstrates the particular targeted behavior, start at 80% compliance. If they earn 80% of the stickers or checkmarks for the week, they should earn the reward. When they consistently accomplish that for two to three weeks, move on to 85% compliance.

I DID IT!

Student: _____ Class: _____ Date: _____

SKILLS	MON	TUE	WED	THU	FRI
I raised my hand to speak.					
I followed verbal and written directions.					
I paid attention in class for 15-20 minutes.					
I did not distract others.					
I completed my classroom work in a timely manner.					

COMMENTS:_____

_____

_____

_____

_____

_____

Parent Signature:_____

72

Take Charge of Stress

When we get mad, scared or worried, our bodies make chemicals from the stress, like the hormone called cortisol. It speeds the heart rate, quickens the breath, increases blood pressure and even boosts the amount of energy supplied to our muscles.

If stress is starting to wear you down, you can...

- ✓ **RUN**

- ✓ **PLAY**

- ✓ **TAKE DEEP BELLY BREATHS**

- ✓ **COUNT BACKWARDS**

- ✓ **LISTEN TO MUSIC**

- ✓ **IMAGINE BEING IN YOUR "FUN AND HAPPY PLACE"**

You can do it!

When I'm upset, I...

Freeze:
I stop what I'm doing and turn away from what's upsetting me.

Count Backwards:
I count slowly backwards from 20.

Belly Breath In:
I breathe in slowly through my nose to the count of 4.*

Belly Breath Out:
I breathe out slowly through my mouth to the count of 4.*

* Place your hand on your belly. Make sure your hand is moving in and out as you breathe.

Homework Daily Plan

SKILLS	MON	TUE	WED	THU	FRI
I handed in all homework assignments for all my classes.					
I brought home all the materials I needed for my homework.					
I earned a grade of B or better on all my quizzes or tests.					
I earned a grade of B or better on a report or project.					
I wrote all my assignments in my planner.					
I finished my homework by 9:00 p.m.					

COMMENTS:

80% Compliance = _____ Checkmarks per week = Celebration/Treat

Resources & Support for Parents and Teachers

1. Learning Disabilities Association of America (LDA)
   www.ldanatl.org
   Phone: 412-341-1515

2. Council for Learning Disabilities (CLD)
   www.council-for-learning-disabilities.org
   Phone: 913-491-1911

3. The University of Kansas Center for Research on Learning
   www.kucrl.org/sim/strategies.shtml
   Phone: 785-864-4780

4. Learning & The Brain
   www.learningandthebrain.com
   Phone: 781-449-4010 X101

5. Council for Exceptional Children
   www.cec.sped.org

6. International Dyslexia Association
   www.eida.org

7. National Center for Learning Disabilities (NCLD)
   www.NCLD.org

8. Understood
   www.understood.org

9. National Association of School Psychologists
   www.nasponline.org
   Phone: 866-331-NASP

10. International Dyslexia Association
    dyslexiaida.org
    Phone: (410) 296-0232

Biographies

Dr. Joyce Holmes served as Executive Director of Exceptional Student Education and Student Services for a student population of 18,000 in Martin County, Florida for 29 years. Her career has included being a teacher, educational consultant, and an adjunct university professor. Her compassionate advocacy for children with special needs has earned her numerous awards, including national recognition as a recipient of the Joleta Reynolds Service to Special Education Award. She earned Bachelor's degrees in Social Psychology and Mental Disabilities, a Master's in Specific Learning Disabilities, and a Specialist degree and Doctorate in Educational Leadership from Florida Atlantic University.

Dr. Patricia Gage has a PhD in Child/School Psychology, and a master's degree in school psychological services from New York University. She received her bachelor's in Elementary Education and Psychology from Hunter College. She has been a practicing school psychologist for thirty years and is the co-founder of a second company, Hang In There, LLC, which writes and produces a series of mini books with parenting tips for new parents. She is a member of the National Association of School Psychologists and the American Psychological Association.

She has been instrumental in developing a number of local programs for children with disabilities, including the Mainstream Instructional & Behavioral Consultation Program for the Martin County School District, Weebiscus for Hibiscus Children's Center, and the Academic Center at The Pine School. She is also the founder of Women In Philanthropy, a women's philanthropic circle that helps to start programs in the community that promote wellness for women and children. She has been instrumental in writing and receiving a number of grants through the Rotary Club of Stuart, which provided equipment for the blind and literacy programs for children, including adding a children's section to the Martin Health System's Cancer Center Library. She was selected Rotarian of the Year 2002-2003 and 2009-2010, and was the Martin County Women of Distinction for 2003 for the business/Professional category chosen by Soroptimist International.

Find her at www.hangnthere.com

Marlo Garnsworthy is a children's book author, illustrator, editor, and teaches Writing for Children's Books and various writing workshops at the Rhode Island School of Design (RISD CE). She works as a freelance editor with Book Editing Associates and various publishers, and is the 1st Place Winner of the 2013 New England SCBWI Poster Illustration Award and the 2014 R. Michelson Galleries Emerging Artist Award Runner-up. She offers editing, illustration, writing, book design, classes, and mentoring.

Find Marlo at www.WordyBirdStudio.com